For Grannie and Grandpa

Sandy Creek, 122 Fifth Avenue, New York, NY 10011

ISBN 978-0-7607-5976-9

Printed and bound in Thailand

7 9 10 8 6

Joanne Partis

Hungry Harry

Sandy Creek

Harry Frog was feeling hungry.
"What's for dinner?" he asked his mom.
"Well, I think you're old enough to look for
your own food now," said Mommy Frog.

"Terrific!" cried Harry, and off
he leaped across the lily pond . . .

till he came to some tall reeds.
"There's sure to be something tasty
here," said Harry, licking his lips.

Sure enough, there was a delicious-looking dragonfly. Harry was just about to jump when . . .

the dragonfly flew off, high
into the air.
"You can't eat me!" she called.
"I'm much too quick for you."

Harry was wondering
what to do next when
suddenly he saw . . .

a big juicy caterpillar
on a twig above him.

"Goody, goody, dinner at last!" cried Harry, but when he flicked out his long tongue to catch it . . .

the caterpillar laughed. "You can't eat me!" she said. "My hairs would tickle your tongue."

"Never mind, I'll find something soon," said Harry.
He bounced on until he met . . .

a scrumptious-looking snail crawling toward him.

"Yummy, yummy," said Harry, but when he reached it . . .

the snail's head suddenly disappeared!
"You can't eat me!" said the
snail from inside its shell.
"I'm much too clever."

Harry was getting hungrier and hungrier.
He was just about to give up and go
home to his mom when he spotted . . .

a squirmy worm, wriggling
along.
"Now's my chance!" cried
Harry, but just as he was
about to catch the worm
in his big wide mouth . . .

it slithered down into a
wormhole.
"You can't eat me!"
shouted the worm. "I'm
too squiggly and squirmy."

Harry felt very fed up. He would go home to his mom. But just as he turned to hop back, he saw something he'd never seen before . . .

It didn't look too quick . . .

It didn't look too tickly . . .

It didn't look too clever . . .

And it didn't look
too squiggly and
squirmy.

In fact it looked . . .

absolutely delicious!

And, what was more . . .

there was eno